My 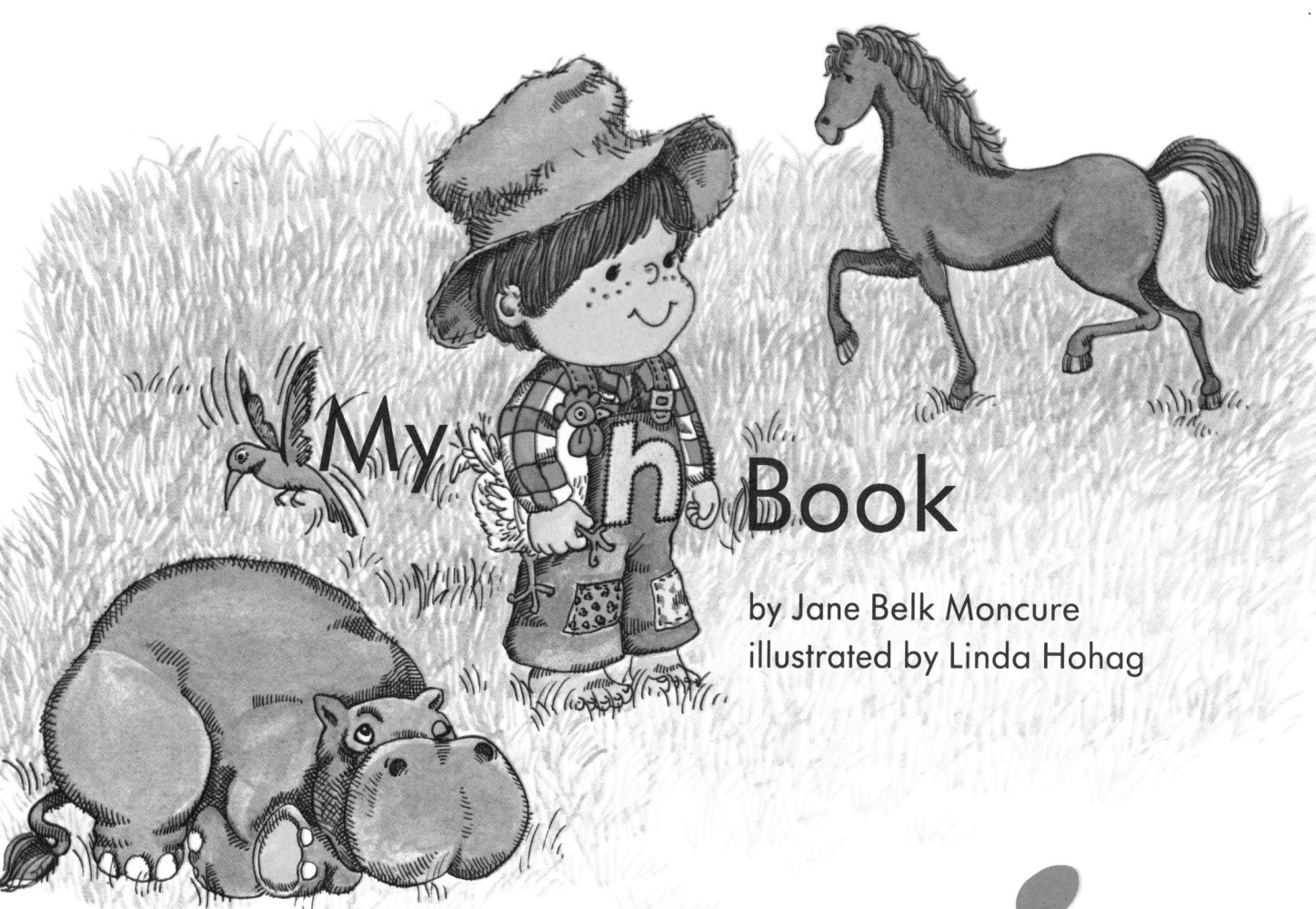h Book

by Jane Belk Moncure

illustrated by Linda Hohag

THE CHILD'S WORLD

Mankato, MN 56001

Little  had a box.

He said, "I will fill my box."

He found hats.

He put on a hat.

He put lots of hats into his box.

8

Little  found a  hen.

"Hi, hen," he said.
"Come into
my box."

9

Then he found a  hog.

box

Into his box
went the hog!

Little  **h** found a
horse.

He hopped on.

The horse
went up the hill.

"Go higher," said Little .

But the horse stopped.
So Little put the horse
into his box.

Then he found a

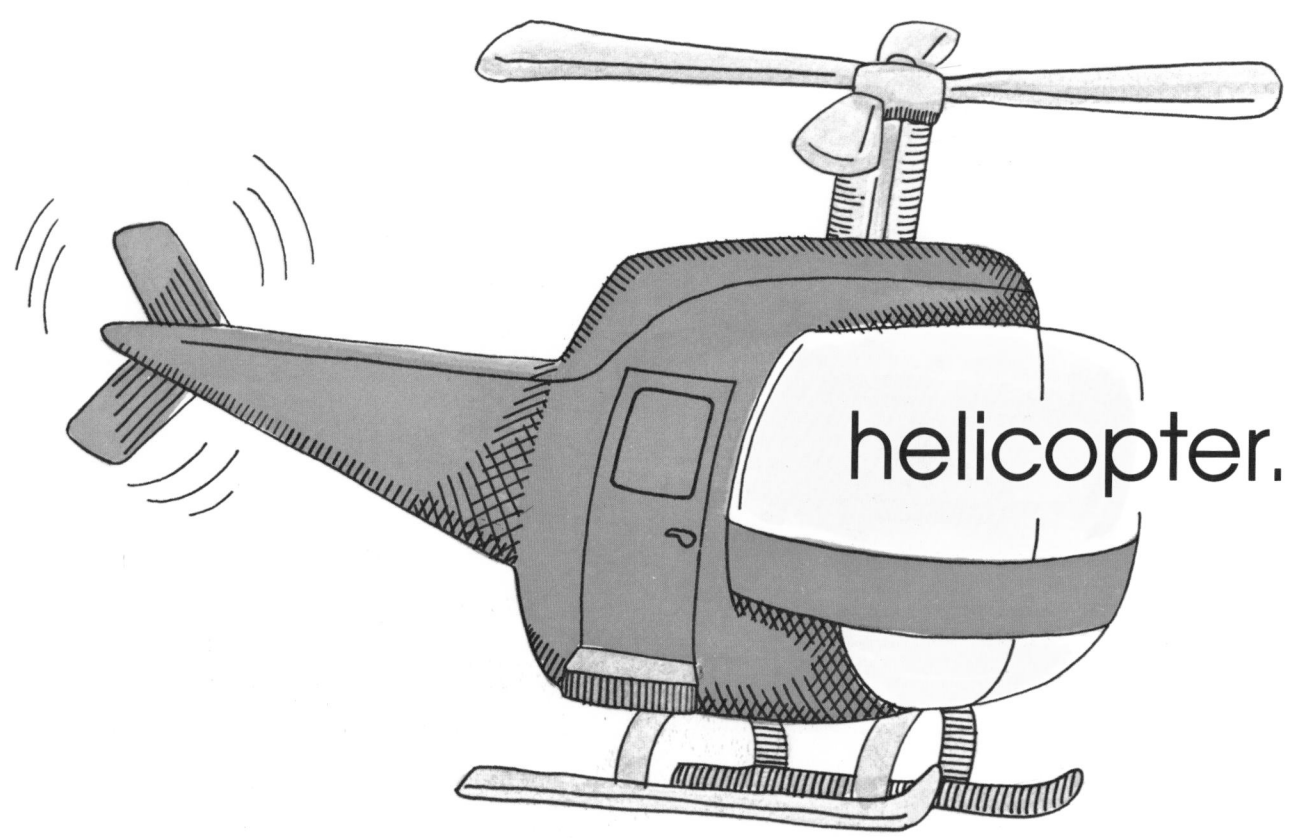

helicopter.

The helicopter could go high.

14

But the helicopter went too high.

"Help!" "Help!" "Help!"

So Little h put it into his box.

Little 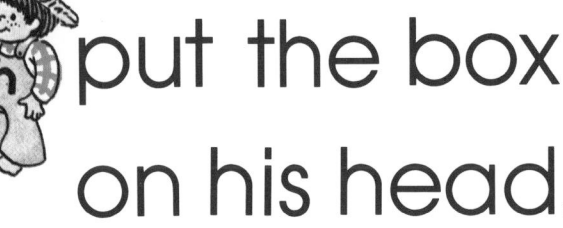 put the box on his head.

box

He did not
see the hole.

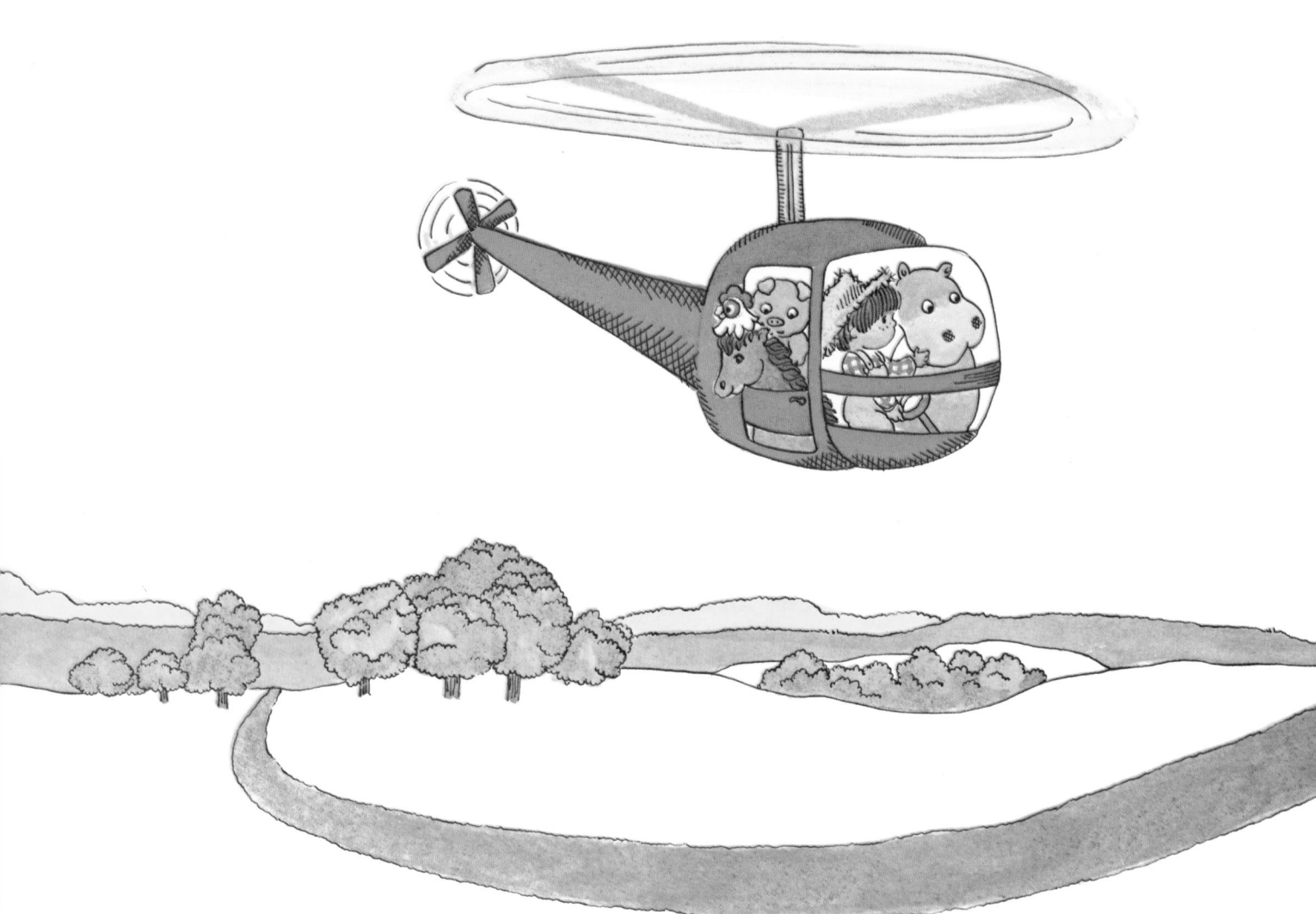

Then they flew up and away...

Little  took the helicopter out of his box.

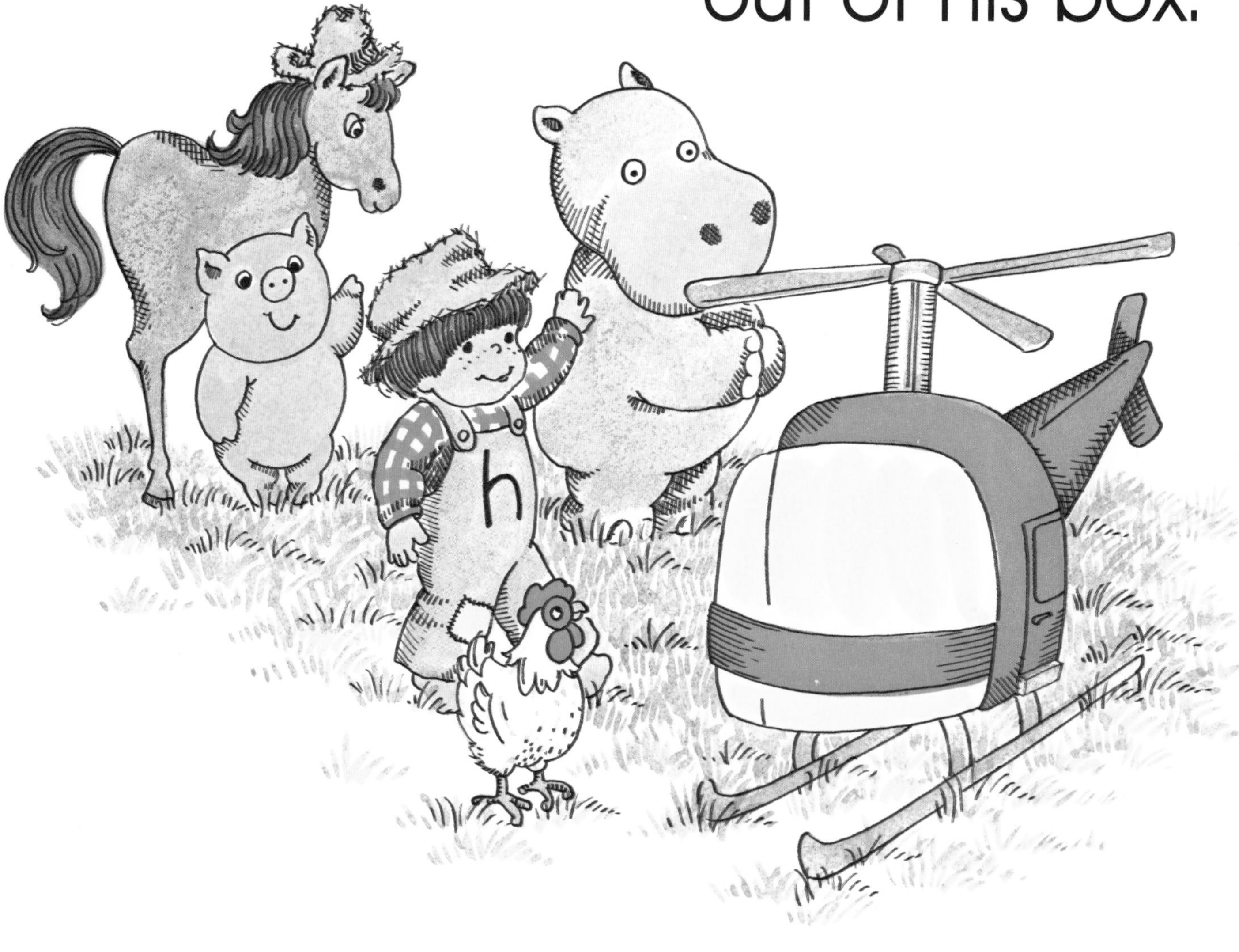

"How can I thank you?"

Little  h asked.

"I like your helicopter," said the hippo.

"How about a ride?"

She helped them out of the hole.

A hippo heard the horn.

Little  **h** had a horn.

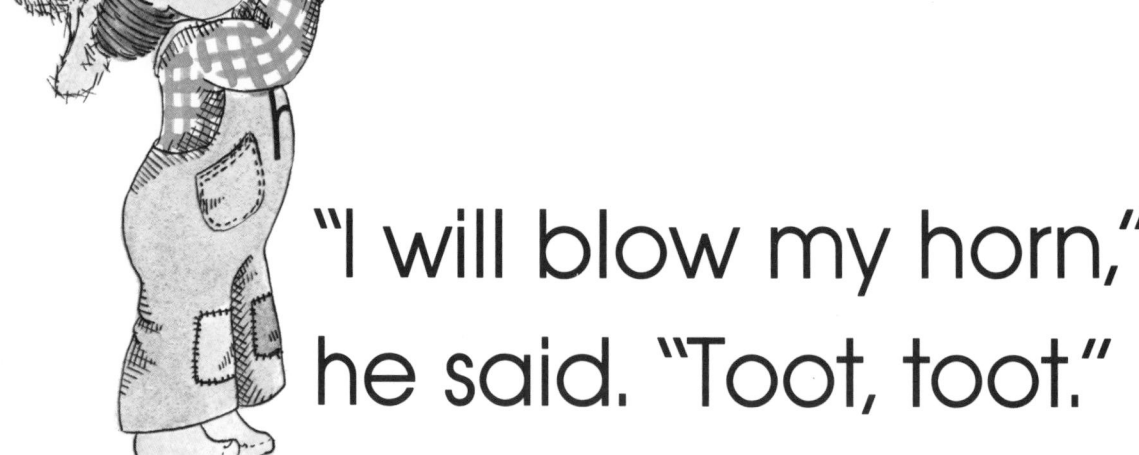 "I will blow my horn," he said. "Toot, toot."